Ziggy's BIG Idea

This tale is dedicated to the memory of Benji and Marina's grandfathers, Charles Long and Martin Blatt, descendants from the shtetl families of Langshtiltsken and Shvartzblatt — I.L.

KAR-BEN PUBLISHING
A division of Lerner Publishing Group, Inc.
241 First Avenue North
Minneapolis, MN 55401 U.S.A.
1-800-4-KARBEN

Website address: www.karen.com

Library of Congress Cataloging-in-Publication Data

Long, Ilana.
    Ziggy's big idea / by Ilana Long ; illustrated by Rasa Joni.
        pages   cm
    Summary: Ziggy is a little boy with a lot of big ideas that have not turned out well, but when Moishe the baker asks him to find a way to make boiled buns that are not undercooked in the center Ziggy is up for the challenge.
        ISBN 978-0-7613-9053-4 (lib. bdg. : alk. paper)
        ISBN 978-1-4677-2428-9 (eBook)
        [1. Inventors—Fiction. 2. Bagels—Fiction. 3. Jews—Fiction.] I. Joni, Rasa, illustrator.
    II. Title.
    PZ7.L8474Zig 2014
    [E]—dc23   2013002191

Manufactured in the United States of America
1 – CG – 12/31/13

Ziggy's BIG Idea

by Ilana Long

illustrated by Rasa Joni

KAR-BEN
PUBLISHING

It was dawn, and the shtetl was still as stone. Even the pigeons waited quietly for the summer day to begin. Morning was Ziggy's favorite time to think up new ideas. Skipping lightly on the cobblestones, he followed his father to the bakery.

"Look at this, Papi." He reached into his pocket and tossed a carved wooden block into the air. "It's my new invention. I call it a Ziggyball."

Papi raised an eyebrow. "That's not a ball. It's a cube."

"Exactly," Ziggy said. "Now it won't roll into the street while I'm playing!"

Papi laughed. Ziggy was always full of unusual ideas.

When they reached the bakery, Papi filled his basket with buns. Like many Jews in the shtetl, Ziggy's father made his living peddling on busy street corners.

"When can I help, Papi?" Ziggy asked for the hundredth time.

"Ah, Ziggeleh! Not until you're older. Now is the time to concentrate on your studies."

"That's right" echoed Moishe the baker. "Study hard when you're young, so when you grow up you can invent something wonderful, like my top secret boiled buns."

Ziggy laughed. Even kids knew the secret behind Moishe's buns. They were first boiled and then baked, making them soft and fluffy inside, and gold and crunchy on the outside.

"Still, there's always room for improvement," Moishe admitted. "Mrs. Schwartz complains that the buns are undercooked at the center." Ziggy didn't say anything, but Papi could tell he was thinking.

Papi took his basket of buns and walked toward the center of town, while Ziggy walked to the shul, where the boys of the shtetl studied Torah. He arrived early, because he had a surprise for the rabbi.

Rabbi Levi was a tiny man. Even on his tippy toes, the top of his hat barely reached Ziggy's nose.

"Rebbe, I made a present for you." Ziggy opened a sack to reveal
two wooden blocks attached to posts. "I call them 'shulstilts.' Now
you'll be able to see your congregation over the bimah!"

"What genius, Ziggy!" the rabbi exclaimed, stepping onto the stilts. "Now, I'll be high enough to read the Torah with ease!

"Now I'll be eye to eye with the bar mitzvah boys! Now I'll be able to –whoops!" And with that, the rabbi tumbled forward, his black hat flying through the air like a dizzy crow.

Ziggy helped the rabbi to his feet.
"Don't worry, Ziggy," said the rabbi. "You have so many
good ideas. I'm sure your next one will be better."

That night, Ziggy fell asleep thinking. In the morning, he hopped out of bed. His imagination had dreamed up his most promising idea yet. He jumped onto Papi's bed in excitement.

"Papi," Ziggy shouted, "I've got it! I have a solution to the baker's problem." Grabbing Papi's hand, Ziggy pulled him out the door.

"Wait!" Papi stopped. "First, I think we should change out of our pajamas."

When Papi and Ziggy arrived, the baker was already preparing the buns. Ziggy raced inside and rubbed his hands with flour.

"So you're the baker now?" Moishe asked.

"I'm just a little boy with a big idea." Ziggy smiled, as he rolled a ball of dough into a wiggly snake. He took the two ends and pinched them together. "Ta-da!" he chimed.

"Aha!" Moishe exclaimed. He took Ziggy's dough circle and carefully placed it into the pot of boiling water. It rose to the top, bobbing like a raft in a stormy sea. The baker scooped it out and put it in the oven, baking it until it was perfectly puffed and beautifully brown.

"Hot! Hot! Hot!" the baker exclaimed, as he took the bun out of the oven. He tossed it from hand to hand to cool and then took a tiny nibble.

"Delicious!" he declared. "And no undercooked center. Ziggy, you're a genius!"

Soon all three of them were working together, rolling the dough, dropping the circles into the boiling water, and then placing them into the oven. Moishe stacked the finished buns on the counter. "My wonderful son!" Papi exclaimed. "Now *that* is a big idea."

Ziggy giggled, as Papi danced the broom around the room. "So, Ziggy, what will you call your new invention?" the baker wondered. Ziggy thought for awhile. He slipped a ring roll over his over his wrist. "That's it!" Ziggy declared. "It's a bracelet; a bagel," he announced. "A perfect name."

"Now watch this!" Ziggy exclaimed, grabbing a broom from the corner.

"First he thinks he's a baker," Papi said, "and now he's the clean-up crew."

"Not for sweeping. For stacking!" Ziggy slipped one bun, then two, then five more onto the broomstick. "Buns on a stick," Ziggy laughed. "Papi, I bet you can easily carry twenty bagels on your walking stick."

Mrs. Schwartz poked her head into the bakery. "What's all the ruckus so early in the morning?"

"You're just in time to try Ziggy's new invention," Papi said. "Please, try a bagel from my broom."

Mrs. Schwartz sniffed the bagel. She nibbled the bagel. She took an enormous bite of the bagel. "This bun is baked perfectly," she announced.

"It's not a bun. It's a bagel!" Ziggy said with pride. And that may be how bagels came to be.

Ziggy's Bagels

1½ cups lukewarm water
1 packet active dry yeast
4 Tbsp. sugar
2 tsp. salt
4 cups flour
1 Tbsp. vegetable oil
2 Tbsp. milk
Sesame seeds (optional)

DIRECTIONS: (Make sure a grown-up is there to help you.)
In a big bowl, mix ¼ cup of the lukewarm water with the yeast, and stir it with a fork. Let it sit for five minutes. Then, add the rest of the lukewarm water, three tablespoons of the sugar and the salt. Next, add two cups of the flour and mix it with your hands. Slowly add more flour until the dough gets thick. Keep mixing while you sing the alphabet song four times. You should be able to make a handprint in your dough when it's ready.

Put the dough onto a floured surface and get your hands all floury. Knead the dough for about ten minutes, adding some more flour if the dough feels sticky. This is a good time to sing some more.

Put the dough in a bowl with a little oil in it. Roll the dough around in the oil to make the outside of the dough ball slippery. Cover it with plastic wrap and put it in a warm, dry place. Let it rise for an hour while you go play.

After the dough has risen, get some more flour on your hands and punch the dough. This is lots of fun. Knead it for a minute.

Ask a grown-up to bring a big pot of water to a boil, with the last tablespoon of sugar in it. Grease your baking pan and have a grown-up preheat the oven to 400 degrees.

Break your dough into eight pieces, and roll each into a wiggly, thick snake. Pinch the ends together to make a "bagel bracelet." Put the bagels on a floured surface and cover loosely with a dry towel. Let them sit for ten minutes.

Ask your grown-up to gently drop the bagels into boiling water and flip them after 30 seconds on each side. You can do this a couple of bagels at a time. Take your bagels out of the pot with a slotted spoon, put them on a towel for a moment, and then plop them onto a greased baking pan.

Brush on the milk, and sprinkle with sesame seeds if you like. Bake the bagels for about 25 minutes until they turn a beautiful, golden color. Yum!

Makes 8 large bagels

ABOUT THE BAGEL

There are conflicting stories about the origin of the bagel. Some say the word comes from the Yiddish word *beygel*, an old German word for a ring or bracelet. Some say it comes from the German word *bügel*, a round loaf of bread. A third legend credits King Jan Sobieski of Poland with bringing about the creation of the bagel. As the story goes, this king abolished a decree limiting the making of bread to the Krakow bakers guild. This meant that Jews could bake and sell bread in the city of Krakow. It said that a Viennese Jewish baker then created a roll in the shape of the king's stirrup and called it a *beugel*, the Austrian word for stirrup.

FUN FACT: Canadian-born astronaut Gregory Chamitoff is the first person known to have taken a batch of bagels into space on his 2008 Space Shuttle mission to the International Space Station.

About the author and illustrator

ILANA LONG is seriously funny. She is an author, stand-up comic, and a middle school English and drama teacher. Ilana studied improvisational comedy at Second City in Chicago. Her love of travel has taken her to many places, including Cancun, Mexico, where she taught high school, and was quickly surpassed by her children in Spanish language acquisition. She lives in the Seattle area with her husband and twin eleven-year-olds.

RASA JONI is a professional book illustrator, as well as a writer, a scriptwriter and an animator. She has worked with publishing houses in South Korea, Italy, Sweden, England and Lithuania, and has published two children's books of her own. She has a doggy and a kitty, who unfortunately, can't draw or paint, but are still good company.